The Case Of The
SCREAMING SCARECROW

Look for more great books in

series:

The Case Of The
SCREAMING SCARECROW

by Judy Katschke

HarperEntertainment
An Imprint of HarperCollinsPublishers

A PARACHUTE PRESS BOOK

PARACHUTE PRESS

Parachute Publishing, L.L.C.
156 Fifth Avenue
New York, NY 10010

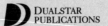

DUALSTAR PUBLICATIONS

Dualstar Publications
c/o Thorne and Company
A Professional Law Corporation
1801 Century Park East
Los Angeles, CA 90067

HarperEntertainment

An Imprint of HarperCollins*Publishers*
10 East 53rd Street, New York, NY 10022

ISBN 0-06-106647-8

HarperCollins®, ■®, and HarperEntertainment™ are trademarks of HarperCollins Publishers Inc.

First printing: September 2001

Printed in the United States of America

mary-kateandashley.com

America Online Keyword: mary-kateandashley

10 9 8 7 6 5 4 3 2 1

1

BIG PLANS

"**G**hosts," Samantha Samuels decided. "We have to have ghosts. Right, Mary-Kate?"

"Definitely," I agreed. "And fake spider-webs, and spooky music, and—"

"Wait a minute," my twin sister, Ashley, said. "Let me write all this stuff down so we don't forget."

The three of us were sitting at the picnic table in Samantha's backyard. In one week we would be having a big Halloween party there. We had a lot of planning to do.

Ashley wrote *ghosts*, *webs*, and *music* in her notebook. She's very organized. I kind of jump into things. Sometimes people expect us to act alike because we look alike. But we're very different.

Ashley likes to stop and think. I follow my feelings. That makes us a good team. Especially when we're solving mysteries. We run the Olsen and Olsen Mystery Agency out of the attic of our house.

But right now we weren't trying to solve anything—except what decorations we wanted for our party!

"How could I forget?" I cried. "We need jack-o'-lanterns with really scary faces!"

"You mean like this?" someone asked. Samantha's older brother, Evan, had walked into the yard. He opened his mouth really wide and crossed his eyes.

Samantha laughed. "You don't look scary. You just look silly."

Evan made another "monster" face. Then he grabbed his football from under the table and ran off.

That's when I noticed a girl with short blond hair on the sidewalk behind the hedge. It was Maggie Parker, a new girl in school.

"Hi, Maggie!" I called. We all waved.

Maggie smiled shyly. "Hi," she said. "What are you doing?"

"We're planning a Halloween party," Samantha explained. "It's going to be huge."

"We're talking about the decorations," Ashley said.

"Decorations?" our friend Patty O'Leary asked. She had just walked up next to Maggie. "For what?"

"We're having a party on Friday, remember?" Samantha said.

"Oh, right," Patty said. Then she frowned. "So why haven't you asked *my*

advice?" she demanded. "I'm an expert party planner!"

I rolled my eyes. Oh, no, I thought. Now Princess Patty is going to try to take over. We call her Princess Patty because she always wants to have her own way.

Patty pushed through a gap in the hedge. Her brown ponytail swung back and forth as she marched toward us.

"Bye," Maggie said. She gave a little wave and walked on toward her house. I guess she was too shy to stay.

Patty plunked her heavy backpack onto the picnic table. Pinned to the flap was a silver-and-purple button. It said FUTURE CEO'S OF AMERICA. That's a new club that Patty started at school.

CEO stands for Chief Executive Officer. Patty likes to brag about how she's going to run a big company someday. But for now, I just knew she was going to try to run our party.

And I was right. Patty wanted to be our CPP—Chief Party Planner. "*Somebody* has to be in charge," she said. "There's tons of stuff to do."

"I know. That's why we're making a list." Ashley held up her notebook.

Patty peered at the list. "*Everybody* has jack-o'-lanterns and fake spiderwebs," she said with a sniff. "Did you see that huge mechanical witch at the Party Shop? It's great! You should get your parents to buy it for you."

Samantha sighed. "We're just going to use regular decorations."

Patty sniffed again. "What about the music? If this were *my* party, I'd hire a band. They could dress in skeleton costumes."

Ashley laughed. "Come on, Patty," she said. "You know we can't pay for a band. But Mary-Kate and I have an old tape of fake screams and spooky music. We can use that."

"Right," I agreed. "And we have some fake spiderwebs, too. All we have to do is buy the pumpkins and candy."

"*And* give out the invitations," Ashley added. She pointed to a tall stack of orange-and-black envelopes on the picnic table. "We invited everyone at school. Too bad Maggie left so fast. We could have given her an invitation right now."

"Here's yours, Patty." I fished one of the envelopes out of the pile and handed it over to her.

"You haven't delivered them yet?" Patty said. She shook her head. "Halloween's only a week away!"

I suddenly had an idea. "Why don't *you* give out the invitations, Patty?" I asked.

Patty shrugged. "Okay. Hey, I have something for you guys." She unzipped her book bag. Inside was a mess of notebooks and papers and pencils. And a bag of black rubber spiders.

Patty pointed to the spiders. "You could use these for decorations," she said.

"No, thanks," I told her. "I'm not crazy about spiders. Even rubber ones."

Patty seemed a little miffed. "Fine," she said. "I'll go deliver the invitations now." She scooped up the envelopes and stuffed them inside her book bag. Then she walked out of the yard.

Ashley sighed. "Well, that should keep Patty busy," she said. "For a while, anyway!"

Later that afternoon Ashley and Samantha and I went to buy pumpkins. Evan came with us, too. A new fruit-and-vegetable stand had just opened up a few blocks away.

All kinds of pumpkins were piled on tables in front of a small wooden hut. Big pumpkins. Tiny pumpkins. In-between pumpkins.

We each picked some out and put them

into Samantha's old red wagon. When we went to pay for them, the owner of the stand stepped out of the hut. He had a round bald head and a missing front tooth. "Making pies, are you?" he asked.

"Jack-o'-lanterns," I told him. "They're going to be decorations for our Halloween party."

"Ah!" the man said. Then he smiled. "Say, I have the perfect decoration for you." He reached back into the hut and brought out—a scarecrow!

The scarecrow was as tall as Evan. It wore overalls, a straw hat, and a green bandanna around its neck.

But the expression on the scarecrow's face was the meanest-looking I'd ever seen! "I bet that really scares the crows," I whispered to Ashley and Samantha.

Samantha shivered. "Yeah. It's so creepy-looking. I feel like it's glaring right at me!"

The owner heard her. "That's what

everyone says," he told us. "Maybe that's why I can't seem to get rid of this scarecrow. People buy it. But they always bring it back."

"Why?" I asked.

The owner lowered his voice. "They all say they've heard it scream—loud enough to scare a ghost! It brings bad luck, they tell me. Some say that the scarecrow is haunted!"

Samantha shivered again.

"Cool," Evan said.

"Well, I don't believe any of that stuff," Ashley said. "But I think the scarecrow would be a perfect decoration for our party."

"Me, too," I said. "I think." That scarecrow still looked pretty creepy to me.

"But we probably can't afford it," Samantha pointed out. She sounded relieved.

"Of course you can," the owner told her. "Like I said, I can't get rid of it. I'll let you have it for free."

"Wow! That's awesome!" Evan said.

"Um, thanks. But I think we have more than enough decorations already," Samantha said quickly.

"You're just scared," Evan teased her. "You think that scarecrow's really haunted."

"No, I don't," Samantha said. She crossed her arms. "Not really."

"Don't worry, Samantha," Ashley said. "There's no such thing as a haunted scarecrow. Think about it."

My sister likes to stop and think. She's always very logical.

"Ashley's right," I said. "And the scarecrow will look great. We could put it right in the middle of the yard."

Samantha glanced back at the scarecrow. "Well…"

"Ha, ha! You *are* scared," Evan teased.

Samantha frowned at him. "I am not."

"Then take it," Evan said. "I dare you."

"Go ahead," the owner urged with a

wink and a nod. "It's a one-time offer."

Samantha stared at the scarecrow for a minute. Finally she nodded. "Okay. We'll take it!"

"Just promise me one thing," the owner said, chuckling. "You won't bring it back!"

When the four of us got back to Samantha's yard, we put the scarecrow in the storage shed and shut the door. Evan went into the house to watch TV.

Ashley, Samantha, and I decided to carve our pumpkins right away. But just as we sat down at the picnic table, we heard a horrible scream!

"Look!" Samantha gasped. She pointed a shaking finger at the storage shed. The scarecrow was glaring at us from the open doorway!

2

BIG TROUBLE

"**A**aahhh!" the scarecrow screamed again.

It shook for a minute, as if it were alive. Then, with a loud rustle, it fell to the ground!

Samantha leaped up from the picnic table. Her brown eyes were frightened. "It *does* scream!" she cried.

"That's impossible," Ashley said.

I jumped up, too. "I don't believe it, either. Come on, Ashley. I have a hunch what's going on."

When Ashley and I solve a case together, she tries to get all the facts. I like to follow my hunches. And this one was too strong to ignore.

We both ran to the shed. Samantha followed us. She still looked scared.

"Look," I said. I pointed to a trail of straw on the floor. It led to the window in the back of the shed.

"I think your hunch is going to pay off, Mary-Kate," Ashley said.

We followed the bits of straw out of the shed. They led all the way to the side door of Samantha's house.

I pulled open the door. We all stepped into the kitchen. "There's your screaming scarecrow, Samantha!" I announced.

I pointed to Evan. He was standing at the counter, munching on an apple.

There was more straw under the table. Two pieces were still stuck to his shoe.

"Your brother hid behind the scarecrow

so it looked like it was standing in the door," I explained. "He screamed a couple of times. Then he dropped it."

"While we were looking at the scarecrow on the ground, he crawled out the shed window and ran in here," Ashley said.

Evan held up his hands. "Okay, I confess." He grinned. "You were sooo freaked, Samantha!"

Samantha frowned at him. "You would have been scared, too. And you'd better not play any more tricks."

"That's right," I added. "Remember, Ashley and I are really good at solving things. If anything else happens, we'll be on your case!"

The next day was Saturday. Ashley and I did some chores. Then we went to Samantha's house to work on the decorations.

First we finished carving our jack-o'-

lanterns. "Did Evan try to play any more tricks with the scarecrow?" I asked.

Samantha shook her head. "Mom told him to leave it alone or he'd get in trouble. But I still wish we hadn't taken that thing. It really gives me the creeps."

I scooped some seeds out of my pumpkin. "I know what you mean," I said. "But Halloween decorations are supposed to be scary."

"Yeah, like this," Ashley said. She held up her jack-o'-lantern. It had tiny, mean-looking eyes. Pumpkin pulp hung from its jagged teeth.

"Now, *that's* creepy!" I said.

We all laughed and finished carving our pumpkins. Then we hung old sheets from tree branches all around the yard. They made great ghosts. Especially when they fluttered in the wind.

I glanced around the yard. "This is going to look so cool when we are finished," I said. "Let's do the spiderwebs next."

"And we need to figure out where to put the scarecrow," Ashley added. "I'll go and get it."

Samantha and I started draping the fake spiderwebs on the bushes. Ashley headed toward the shed.

"Hi!" Patty called over the hedge. She pushed through the branches and stepped into the backyard. "I delivered all the invitations," she announced.

"Great. Thanks, Patty," I said. "We just finished carving our pumpkins. Don't they look cool?"

Patty came over to the picnic table. She pointed to my jack-o'-lantern. "That one's mouth is crooked," she said.

I gritted my teeth. Sometimes Patty could be so rude.

"And you only have five pumpkins," Patty went on.

I rolled my eyes. "You didn't think we

should have *any*," I reminded her.

"Well, if you're going to have them, you should have *lots* more than five," she replied. "If this were my party, I'd have dozens."

This wasn't Patty's party. But that didn't stop her from trying to take over.

She pointed to the sheets we'd hung from the trees. "Let me guess—those are supposed to be ghosts, right?"

"Yes," Samantha said.

"What else could they be?" I asked.

"Laundry!" Patty laughed.

I sighed. Patty was being a real pain.

"And those spiderwebs," Patty said. "They're so ugly! Why don't you get rid of all this stuff and start over?"

Just then, Ashley came out of the shed carrying the scarecrow.

Patty gasped. "What on earth is that... that...*thing?*"

"This?" Ashley put the scarecrow up

against an oak tree in the middle of the yard. "It's a scarecrow. The man at the pumpkin stand gave it to us for free."

"And you took it?" Patty asked. She wrinkled her nose.

Ashley shrugged. "Hey, it looks great."

"Well, at least it's not boring," Patty said. "Like all the other decorations."

"Well *we* like them," I told her. "And I bet everybody else will, too."

"Mary-Kate's right," Samantha agreed. "Stop picking on everything, Patty."

Patty looked insulted. "I'm just trying to help."

"You helped already," I said. "You delivered the invitations."

"You mean you don't want me to do anything else?" Patty frowned.

"Not if you're going to be so bossy," Ashley said.

"Well, fine!" Patty replied. She was so mad her face turned red. "But if I hadn't given out those invitations, nobody would even know about your stupid party. And your decorations *are* boring!"

Patty stormed out of the yard. When she got to the other side of the hedge, she stopped. "You're going to be sorry!" she hollered. "Because without my help this party's going to be a total disaster. Just wait and see!"

3

THE SCARECROW STRIKES AGAIN

"Uh-oh," I said to Ashley and Samantha. "Patty is really mad at us."

Samantha bit her lip. "I wonder if she'll still come to the party." Samantha looked unhappy. She doesn't like to fight, even with Patty.

"Don't worry, Samantha," Ashley said. "If everybody else comes, I bet Patty will, too."

I nodded. "Patty hates to be left out."

"I guess you're right," Samantha said slowly.

"Come on," I said. "Let's keep working on the *boring* decorations!"

Ashley and I went home for dinner. Then we walked back to Samantha's house. She had invited us to spend the night.

But as we stepped onto the porch, Samantha threw open the front door. "Something really weird is going on!" she said. She looked really upset.

"What do you mean?" I asked.

"It's the scarecrow," Samantha replied. "It keeps moving around. It was in the yard when you left. But when I came outside after dinner, it was sitting at the picnic table. And later I found it in my bedroom!"

Ashley and I looked at each other. "Evan!" we said at the same time.

Samantha shook her head. "Not this time. He went to the park with some friends."

"Are you sure he was gone the whole time?" Ashley asked.

"No," Samantha admitted. "But I didn't see any pieces of straw like we did before."

"That's because Evan probably picked them up," I said. "Where is the scarecrow now?"

"I put it back in the shed," Samantha said.

"Let's go check it out," Ashley said. "I bet we'll find some clues to prove it was Evan."

"Like footprints?" Samantha asked.

"Exactly," I said, nodding. "Or maybe something fell out of his pocket and he didn't notice it."

"This shouldn't be a hard mystery to solve," Ashley said.

"I hope not," Samantha declared. She shivered. "I still don't like that scarecrow."

The three of us walked around the side of the house to the backyard. It was dark. But we could see the white-sheet ghosts flapping in the breeze.

"Those ghosts look really spooky!" Ashley said.

"Yeah, *too* spooky," Samantha whispered. "Come on, let's hurry!"

We ran to the shed and pulled open the door. Ashley and I took our flashlights out of our backpacks and turned them on.

"Do you see anything?" Samantha asked nervously from behind us.

"Nope," Ashley said.

"No clues at all?" Samantha asked.

"No scarecrow," I replied.

Samantha peered inside the shed. "But I put it back here just a little while ago!" she said.

"Well, the scarecrow didn't leave by itself," Ashley said. "Come on, let's go find your brother."

"He's not home," Samantha told us as we walked toward the house. "He went next door with Mom and Dad to see the neighbors' new big-screen TV."

"That doesn't give him a perfect alibi," I said. An alibi is a reason someone couldn't have done something. "Evan could have sneaked over here and moved the scarecrow. Then he could have run back to the neighbors' house."

"Mary-Kate's right," Ashley agreed. "I bet Evan had plenty of chances. *And* he had a motive—he likes to tease you."

Alibis and motives are super important when you're solving a mystery. But I still didn't think this was much of a mystery. Evan *had* to be the culprit.

We went into the kitchen. The scarecrow wasn't there. Neither was Evan.

"Let's check out the rest of the house," Ashley suggested. "Maybe Evan put the scarecrow in here somewhere."

We walked through the kitchen toward the stairs. Suddenly we heard a horrible scream. "AAAAHHH!"

"That came from the front of the house!" I cried.

We rushed down the hall to the living

room. Samantha stopped in the doorway. "L-look!" she stammered. "Look out the window!"

Right outside the window was a weird shadow in the shape of a person. It made a rustling sound as it swayed back and forth. "AAAHHH!" the chilling scream came again.

"It's the scarecrow!" Samantha cried. She turned to run and bumped into Ashley. Ashley bumped into me, and I bumped into the wall.

We all fell in a heap. By the time we got up, the shadow had disappeared.

"Come on, you guys!" Ashley cried. "If we hurry, we can catch him!"

"I don't want to catch that scarecrow!" Samantha said.

"Ashley meant we can catch Evan," I explained.

We hurried out the front door. The porch was empty. No scarecrow. No Evan. We ran down the steps to the sidewalk.

"AAHH…AAAHHHRGH!"

The three of us jumped and spun around.

The scarecrow was standing in the doorway behind us!

4

Bad Rubbish

Samantha and I screamed. So did Ashley—and she hardly ever screams. We couldn't help it. Having the scary-looking scarecrow turn up like that was just plain freaky!

The three of us ran in different directions. We all ended up in the backyard, out of breath.

"I can't believe that thing scared me like that," I said.

But Ashley didn't answer. She was busy

staring at the shed. "The door is open," she said. "I *know* I closed it when we went into the house."

"Let's check it out," I said.

We hurried to the shed. Even though we didn't have our flashlights, we could see that something was different. Very different.

The scarecrow was back!

We hardly slept all night. All of us were thinking about the scarecrow. How could it keep moving around like that—all by itself? It just wasn't possible.

After breakfast the next morning Samantha made an announcement. "I'm taking the scarecrow back to the pumpkin stand."

"Oh, no! Why?" Ashley asked. "I know we didn't get to question Evan last night. He got home too late. But it had to be him playing tricks on us."

"Yeah, Samantha," I said. "Your parents

said he was in and out of the neighbors' house. He could have sneaked over here lots of times."

"I'm positive that's what happened," Ashley agreed. "Leave it to Mary-Kate and me, Samantha. We'll get to the bottom of this. Then we can keep the scarecrow for the party."

It had been too late and dark to do much detecting the night before. But now Ashley and I were ready to figure things out.

"I don't want to keep that scarecrow," Samantha insisted. "Maybe it *was* my brother. Maybe not. But no matter what, that scarecrow is nothing but trouble!"

Ashley and I looked at each other. We didn't want to argue with Samantha. And we didn't want to ruin the party for her if she was that scared of the scarecrow.

We got the scarecrow from the shed. Then the three of us walked to the pumpkin stand.

But the stand was closed. There were no pumpkins. No tables. And the little shed was boarded up.

"It looks as if this place is closed for good," I said.

"But that doesn't make sense," Ashley said. "Halloween isn't here yet. Lots of people will still want to buy pumpkins. Why would the owner close his stand so early?"

A cold wind blew down the street. A shiny black crow perched on top of the shed and glared down at us. "Cawww—cawww!"

"Let's go," Samantha said with a shiver.

"What about the scarecrow?" Ashley asked. "We can't just leave it here. I guess we'll have to keep it."

"No way," Samantha declared. "Remember that big Dumpster we passed on the way here? *That's* where we'll leave the scarecrow."

"You mean you want to throw the scarecrow away?" I asked in surprise. "In the garbage?"

Samantha nodded. "Exactly. Like I said, it's nothing but trouble!"

THE SCREAMING CLUE

"**O**ne...two...three!" Samantha called. On the count of three, she and Ashley and I swung the scarecrow up and over the side of the green Dumpster.

Crash! The scarecrow landed with a loud rustle of straw.

"There!" Samantha wiped her hands and grinned. "It's gone. I feel better already!" She hurried away from the Dumpster.

As Ashley and I followed Samantha down the street, I glanced back. I could see that one of the scarecrow's arms was caught on the edge of the Dumpster.

"It looks like it's trying to climb out," I murmured to my sister.

"Don't tell that to Samantha!" Ashley whispered back. "That scarecrow really has her spooked."

"I was a little scared, too, last night," I admitted.

Ashley nodded. "Well, we both know for sure that the scarecrow didn't run around by itself. All we have to do is find some clues to prove it."

When we got back to Samantha's house, Ashley ran inside to get her notebook. "I'll be right back," she said.

When we're working on a mystery, Ashley likes to make notes. She says it helps her think more clearly. I usually use a tape recorder for my notes, but I didn't have it with me.

As Samantha and I waited on the front porch, I glanced around. "We're in the same spot where the scarecrow was swinging outside the window yesterday," I said.

"Don't remind me," Samantha said.

I searched the porch for footprints, but there weren't any. Then I glanced up. "Samantha, look!"

I pointed to a spot above the living room window. Stuck on a shingle was a little piece of red cloth. "That looks like it came from the scarecrow's shirt!" I said.

I pointed farther up, to a window above the living room. "What room is that?" I asked.

"Evan's bedroom!" Samantha replied.

"Aha!" I cried.

Samantha and I ran inside and up the stairs. Ashley was just coming out of Samantha's room with her notebook. I told her about the piece of cloth.

"We have our first clue," I said. "And I bet it won't be the last!"

We hurried down the hall to Evan's

room. When Samantha knocked on the door, it swung open. Evan wasn't there. But something else was—another clue!

I pointed to the bed. Poking out from underneath it was part of a rope. "There's the answer to the swinging scarecrow," I said.

Ashley pulled the rope all the way out. Another piece of the red cloth was caught on it.

"I don't even have to write this down," Ashley said. "It's easy to tell what happened. Evan lowered the scarecrow out of his window on the rope."

"And he pulled it back up just before we ran outside," I added. "Then he hurried downstairs and propped it in the front door behind us. When we ran, he took it back to the shed."

"And I bet this is how he made the scarecrow scream." Ashley picked up a pocket-size tape recorder from Evan's desk. She pressed the Play button.

"AAARRRGGGHHH!" the recorder shrieked. It was the same horrible scream, all right.

"He must have put the recorder in the scarecrow's shirt pocket when he hung it out the window," Ashley said.

"ARRRGGGGHHH!" the scream came again.

Ashley stopped the tape and took it out. "*Screams, Shrieks, and Other Frightful Sounds*," she read from the label.

"Hey!" Evan cried. He and Mrs. Samuels were standing in the doorway. "What are you doing in my room?"

Ashley held out the tape. I picked up the rope. "Looking for clues," I said. "And we found them."

"Mary-Kate and Ashley figured out how you fooled us last night, Evan," Samantha told him.

The three of us explained everything

that had happened. When we finished, Mrs. Samuels crossed her arms. "I told you not to play any more tricks on the girls, Evan."

"It was just a joke," Evan protested. "I didn't know they were going to throw the stupid scarecrow away!"

"That doesn't matter. I said no jokes," his mother replied. "Now, I want you to help the girls get ready for their party. And no trick-or-treating for you on Friday."

Mrs. Samuels left.

Wow, I thought. *That's pretty harsh.*

Evan gave us all a dirty look. "Thanks a lot, you guys!" he said angrily. "My Halloween is ruined now. And it's all your fault!"

6

SUSPICIOUS SIGNS

"**H**ey, Samantha," Zach Jones said at school the next day. "I got the invitation to your party."

"Me, too," Jeremy Burns said. "It sounds cool."

Our friend Tim Parks just nodded. It was lunchtime and Tim's mouth was too full of food to talk.

"Well, it looks like all our friends got their invitations," Ashley said to me and Samantha.

I nodded and glanced around the big table in the cafeteria. All the kids we'd invited were there, including Maggie and Patty.

"Look at the frown on Patty's face," I murmured. "I guess she's still mad at us."

"So is Evan," Samantha said, pointing to another table. "*Really* mad. He says it's all our fault that he's in trouble."

Tim swallowed the last bite of his cheese-and-pickle sandwich. "Why is your brother in trouble?" he asked.

"Because he played a mean trick with the scarecrow after Mom told him not to," Samantha replied.

"What scarecrow?" Jeremy asked.

Patty sniffed. "It's a ratty old thing they're using for a decoration."

"Well, we're not using it anymore," Samantha told her.

"Good," Patty said. "You finally decided to take my advice."

Ashley shook her head. "Not exactly. We're not using it because—"

"Because we threw it in a Dumpster near my house," Samantha said.

"That big green one on Maple Street?" Maggie asked.

I nodded.

Tim looked surprised. "Why did you get rid of the scarecrow?"

Samantha and Ashley and I told all our friends the whole story.

"You mean you thought that ugly thing was haunted?" Patty sneered.

"Of course not," I said quickly.

"Well…maybe it wasn't," Samantha said. "But it *was* really scary. Besides, the pumpkin man told us it brought bad luck. And it did."

"Yeah, for Evan!" Zach laughed.

"For me, too," Samantha told him. "Evan's really mad at me now, and that's no fun. But I'm glad we got rid of the scarecrow. It was way too spooky."

"I liked it." Ashley sighed. "But we don't really need it."

"Ashley's right," I agreed. "The party will be great without it."

The bell rang. Lunch was over and everyone got up. Patty came up to Ashley, Samantha, and me.

"Maybe you got rid of the scarecrow, but your bad luck isn't over," Patty warned. "Your party's going to be a big flop. Just remember, I told you so!"

Samantha looked sad as Patty stalked away.

"Don't pay any attention to her, Samantha," I said. "She's just mad because we didn't let her be the boss. She'll get over it before the party."

"Right," Ashley agreed. "Let's go shopping after school and buy the candy, okay?"

When school was over, we stopped at a little store in our neighborhood. It sells candy and party decorations. We bought jawbreakers, bubble gum, mini–chocolate bars, lollipops—all kinds of candy.

"Ashley and I have a big plastic skull that we used as a decoration last Halloween," I said as we walked to Samantha's house. "We could put the candy in it and let kids grab it."

"Great idea," Samantha said. Then she pointed to a yellow house on the corner. "Look, there's Maggie's house. Don't those rubber spiders look cool?"

Small black rubber spiders dangled on strings from the roof of Maggie's porch. "Really cool," I said. "If you like spiders."

We kept walking and admiring all the neighbors' Halloween decorations. When we got to Samantha's, we decided to make a sign for our party.

First we cut a big ghost out of some white cardboard. Then, across the front of the ghost, we wrote WELCOME TO OUR

PARTY—HAVE A SCARY GOOD TIME! in green paint.

Below the words we drew a big green arrow pointing to the backyard. Then we stuck the sign on a tree near the front of Samantha's house.

The next morning at our house Ashley and I filled the big plastic skull with candy. We decided to take it to Samantha's house before school. Then the three of us could all walk to the bus together.

"Maybe we shouldn't have left our sign out last night," I said to Ashley. "What if it had rained?"

Ashley stopped in the middle of the sidewalk. "Oh, no!" she cried. "Forget rain, Mary-Kate!"

"What do you mean? What's wrong?" I asked. I hurried after Ashley into Samantha's front yard. Then I saw our sign.

Thick slashes of black and orange paint were smeared all over the white cardboard.

The green letters were totally wiped out. Underneath them, in black, were the words BEWARE—YOUR PARTY IS DOOMED!

"I can't believe this," Ashley said. She pointed to the ground around the tree. "Straw!"

My sister was right. Three pieces of straw lay on the grass. She carefully picked them up.

"They have drops of orange and black paint on them!" I said, frowning.

"Mary-Kate! Ashley!" Samantha ran toward us from the backyard. "Something awful has happened!"

"We know," I said. I pointed to the sign.

When Samantha saw the sign, her eyes got really big. "Oh, no! I didn't even see the sign yet. I was talking about our jack-o'-lanterns!"

We all ran to the backyard. The jack-o'-lanterns were still sitting on the picnic table where we left them. But now they

48

were covered with shiny black paint!

"The party's ruined!" Samantha cried.

"No, it's not," Ashley declared. "But it looks like somebody wants it to be."

"Yeah. The question is *who?*" I said.

I set the plastic skull down next to the pumpkins. Luckily, I had my tape recorder with me this time. I pulled it out of my backpack and clicked it on.

"Eight-ten, Tuesday morning," I said in a low voice. "Ashley and I are at Samantha Samuels's house. Someone has wrecked our Halloween party sign and all our jack-o'-lanterns."

While I was talking, I kept glancing around the yard. So did Ashley. We were looking for clues. Suddenly Ashley bent over and picked something up from the grass.

"Straw!" Samantha said.

Ashley nodded. "With black and orange paint on it. Just like the pieces of straw

Mary-Kate and I saw under the sign."

Ashley held out the straw she'd picked up in the front yard.

Samantha's eyes grew wide again. "The scarecrow!" she cried. "It's stuffed with straw, right? That's where those pieces came from. It's true! The scarecrow really *is* haunted!"

7

THE MAIN SUSPECTS

"**N**o way," Ashley declared. "Stop and think, Samantha. The straw probably just fell out of the scarecrow when we were carrying it around."

I'm glad my sister is always so logical, because I felt a little spooked, too! But I told myself the culprit had to be a real person.

"I bet whoever did this didn't even notice the straw," Ashley said.

"But who would want to wreck our party?" Samantha asked. "Oh, wait a minute! Evan might have done it."

"He's definitely suspect number one," I agreed. "And I already thought of number two—Patty."

Ashley nodded. "Evan blames us because he's in trouble. And Patty's mad because we didn't let her boss us around. She even predicted that the party would be a disaster."

"So maybe she's trying to make her prediction come true," I said.

Samantha frowned. "I know Patty can be mean. But do you really think she would ruin our decorations?"

"That's what the Olsen and Olsen Mystery Agency is going to find out," I told her. I checked my watch. "We have ten more minutes before we have to catch the bus. Let's go talk to Suspect Number One first."

We ran into the house. Evan was eating some cereal at the kitchen table.

Samantha told him about the signs and

the jack-o'-lanterns. "If you did it, you're going to be in even bigger trouble," she declared.

"I didn't do it!" Evan insisted. "Mom just woke me up fifteen minutes ago. It's too bad about your decorations. But I didn't wreck them!"

Evan jumped up from the table and left the kitchen.

"Do you believe him?" Samantha asked Ashley and me.

"He sounded like he was telling the truth," I admitted. "But he still has a motive."

"And no alibi," Ashley added. "He could have wrecked the decorations during the night. Or this morning, before your mom woke him up."

"That means he's still a suspect," I said. "But so is Patty. Let's see what she has to say."

Whoever ruined the sign and the jack-o'-

lanterns could have done it yesterday, during the night, or early this morning.

So we needed to find out Patty's alibi for those times. When we got to school, I tried to talk to her. But she just gave me a dirty look.

"Patty wouldn't speak to me," I told Ashley and Samantha at lunch. "We don't know if she has an alibi. So she's still a suspect."

Ashley jotted it down in her notebook. "We might have a third suspect," she said.

"Who?" Samantha asked in surprise.

Ashley nodded at the table next to ours. "Maggie," she murmured. "She has black and orange paint on her fingers."

I looked. Ashley was right about the paint. "But we were making Halloween pictures in art class this morning," I said. "Maggie might have gotten the paint on her fingers then."

"I thought of that, too," Ashley said.

"And why would Maggie want to wreck our party?"

We couldn't think of any reason. But we didn't cross Maggie off our list. Good detectives have to consider every possibility.

After school Ashley and I walked home with Samantha to help make another sign. "I'm going to keep this one in my room until the night of the party," Samantha declared.

"Good idea," I told her. "And let's get some more pumpkins tomorrow. It won't be Halloween without jack-o'-lanterns."

"I know—I'll get Evan to help carve them," Samantha said. "After all, Mom said he had to help with the party."

"Uh-oh. There's Evan now." Ashley pointed toward Samantha's front yard. "And he still looks mad."

But Evan wasn't mad. He was upset. "Something really weird happened," he told us. "I don't know who did it, but it sure wasn't me!"

"What are you talking about?" Samantha asked.

"Come on—it's in the backyard," he said.

We ran to the back and stopped, totally shocked.

Our sheet ghosts hung from the trees in long, raggedy strips.

"They're shredded!" Samantha cried.

"And check this out!" Evan said. He grabbed the plastic skull and stuck his hand inside. But instead of candy, he brought up a handful of black spiders!

"Those aren't real, are they?" I asked with a shiver.

Evan shook his head. "Rubber."

"What about the candy?" Ashley asked. "That skull was filled with all kinds of candy."

"There's no candy in this skull anymore," Evan told her. "There are some pieces of straw in here, but nothing else."

"Straw?" Samantha cried.

Evan nodded. "There's straw on the ground, too. Little piles of straw under the ghosts. It's kind of creepy."

Samantha stared at Ashley and me. "It's very creepy!"

"Yeah, well, just remember—I didn't do it," Evan repeated. He put the skull down and went inside.

I peered into the skull. Yuck! I didn't even like *looking* at spiders. But they did give me an idea.

"I just remembered something!" I said. "That day we gave Patty the invitations, she had a bag of rubber spiders in her backpack."

"And I just remembered those rubber spiders hanging from Maggie's porch," Ashley told me. She frowned. "But we don't have a motive for Maggie."

"Well, we have one for Patty," I said.

"And Evan, too. He *acted* upset. But he could have been pretending."

Ashley nodded. "It looks like we still have three suspects."

"You guys are forgetting about this." Samantha walked to one of the ghosts and picked up a handful of straw from the ground. "What about the scarecrow?"

"Oh, Samantha, you don't really think the scarecrow is haunted, do you?" Ashley asked. "It's just a bunch of straw and cloth sitting in a Dumpster."

"Hey, why don't we go there now?" I suggested. "The garbage won't be picked up until Friday. So the scarecrow will still be in the Dumpster."

Samantha and Ashley agreed. We left the yard and started walking down the street.

I didn't want to admit it, but those little piles of straw kind of spooked me, too. I would definitely be glad to see that the scarecrow was still where we left it.

When we reached the Dumpster, we grabbed hold of the edge. We pulled ourselves up and peered inside.

Ashley stared. Samantha and I gasped.

The scarecrow was gone!

8

PANIC BUTTON

"**W**here is it?" Samantha asked nervously.

Ashley shook her head. "It's hard to believe," she said. "But the scarecrow seems to have disappeared."

"It *is* haunted!" Samantha cried. "It's getting back at us because we threw it away."

Ashley and I jumped down, too. I didn't blame Samantha for being scared. "Something weird is definitely going on," I admitted.

"I told you. The scarecrow is out for revenge," Samantha insisted. "What are we going to do now?"

"We're going to get to the bottom of this case," Ashley declared. "Come on, Mary-Kate. Let's see if we can find any clues."

Ashley checked the ground around the Dumpster. I found a long stick and climbed back up. I poked the stick around inside the garbage. There were a few pieces of straw, but no other sign of the scarecrow.

"This Dumpster really stinks!" I held my nose as I poked at a garbage bag. "This isn't the fun part of being a detective."

"No, but *this* is!" Ashley cried. "Look what I found!"

I jumped back down. Ashley was holding something in her hand. Something silver and purple—with the words FUTURE CEO'S OF AMERICA printed on it.

"That's Patty's button!" Samantha said. "The one she had pinned to her backpack."

Ashley grinned. "I knew there had to be an explanation. Patty must be our culprit."

I nodded. "She heard us telling everyone at lunch that we threw the scarecrow away. So she decided to take it. And when she wrecked our decorations, she left those pieces of straw on purpose."

"That way we would think the scarecrow had done it," Ashley said. "She wanted to scare us."

"Case closed," I declared. "Except for one thing."

"Right," Ashley agreed. "We have to tell Patty we know what she did!"

We hurried down the block. Patty was in her front yard stringing little jack-o'-lantern lights on the bushes. "What do *you* want?" she demanded when she saw us.

Ashley held out the CEO button. "We found this by the Dumpster," she said.

Patty frowned. "That's not my button," she said. "And besides, I wouldn't go anywhere near that smelly Dumpster."

"You would if you wanted to scare us and wreck our party," Samantha told her.

"I don't know what you're talking about," Patty said. She crossed her arms.

"Come on, Patty," Ashley said. "We know you're mad because we didn't listen to you about the decorations. So you painted over our sign."

"And our jack-o'-lanterns," I added. "You cut up the sheet ghosts, too. And dumped all those rubber spiders in the skull."

"*And* you left all that straw around so I'd think the scarecrow did it," Samantha said.

"You took the scarecrow out of the Dumpster in case we looked for it." Ashley held out the button again. "But you left a teeny, tiny clue. And we found it."

"Stop!" Patty cried, throwing up her hands. "You mean you think *I* did all that stuff?"

"Yes!" the three of us said together.

"Well, you guys are all wrong!" Patty said. "That button isn't mine. And I can prove it!"

Patty marched onto her porch. She grabbed her backpack from one of the chairs. Then she marched back down to us.

"For your information, the pin on *my* button broke," Patty said. She unzipped her backpack and began taking out papers and notebooks and pencils. "I didn't want to lose it. So I put it in here. See?"

Patty pulled out another CEO button and held it up. It looked exactly the same. Then she turned it over. We could see that the pin was broken.

I glanced at Ashley. "Oops. I guess this case isn't closed after all."

"That's for sure," Patty said. "I can't believe you accused me of ruining your decorations. I mean, I was mad. But not *that* mad. Besides, I'm not the only one in the CEO club. Joey and Zach and Stacy are in it, too. And Maggie just became a member."

I looked at Ashley again. "Maggie Parker?" I asked. "The new girl?"

Patty nodded. "I invited her to join. And everybody who joins gets a button. But she's *way* too shy. I don't think she has what it takes to run a company someday."

"But she might have what it takes to be our culprit," Ashley said slowly. "She heard all about the scarecrow, too. I saw orange and black paint on her fingers. And we know she has rubber spiders on her porch."

"The only thing she *doesn't* have is a motive," I reminded my sister.

"That's right," Samantha agreed. "Like Ashley always says, it's not logical. Why would Maggie want to spoil a party she's invited to?"

Ashley's mouth dropped open. "I know why!" she said. "It's because she *wasn't* invited!"

SETTING THE TRAP

"Maggie wasn't invited? What do you mean?" I asked.

"Of course she was invited!" Patty insisted. "I delivered all the invitations myself. Remember?"

"All but one," Ashley told her. She pointed to Patty's backpack.

The corner of an orange envelope was poking out from between some papers. Ashley reached down and pulled it out of the backpack.

"It's Maggie's invitation!" Samantha cried. "She never got it!"

Patty looked embarrassed. "It must have gotten mixed up with all my other stuff," she admitted. "I didn't leave Maggie out on purpose!"

Patty didn't exactly say she was sorry. But I could tell she felt terrible. At least, a little. "We know you didn't do it on purpose," I told her quickly.

"Thanks." Patty started shoving the papers back into her backpack. "So what are you going to do about Maggie?"

"Well, we have a motive for her now," Ashley said. "But we shouldn't accuse her unless we're sure."

"Yeah, like you accused *me*," Patty reminded her.

I rolled my eyes. Things were back to normal with Patty!

"We're really sorry about jumping to conclusions," Ashley said. Ashley, Samantha, and I said good-bye and left Patty's house.

"We need to come up with a plan," Ashley said as we walked down the sidewalk. "If Maggie is the culprit, we have to prove it."

"Right," I agreed. "And the best way is to catch her in the act!"

The next night the three of us slipped into Samantha's backyard. We had already put our plan into motion. Now it was time to see if it worked!

At school that day Ashley and I told everyone about the great new decorations we had made. Skeletons and bats and a giant ghost.

We hadn't really made them. But Maggie didn't know that. And we made sure she heard every word we said!

If Maggie really was the culprit, we were sure she would try to ruin the "new" decorations.

All we had to do now was wait and see.

Samantha hid in the shed. Ashley stood in the shadows of a tree by the back door. I crouched down behind some bushes.

I shivered. It was cold and creepy out in the yard. I hoped something happened soon!

A few minutes went by.

I peeked over the bushes. The yard was still empty. I crouched back down and shivered again.

A few more minutes went by.

Suddenly I heard a rustling sound. Was it the leaves blowing in the wind? I held my breath and listened.

The rustling grew louder. Then I heard footsteps. It's not the wind, I thought. It's Maggie!

As quietly as possible, I peeked over the bushes again—and saw a shadow!

I gulped. My heart started pounding. Because the shadow wasn't Maggie's. Even for a shadow, it was way too tall. And it rustled with every step it took.

It was the dark, creepy shadow of the scarecrow—and it was moving across the backyard!

AN OPEN AND SHUT CASE

I screamed. Samantha screamed.

"Aaahh!" The scarecrow screamed, too. Then, with a rustle of straw, it crashed to the ground. I could see the scarecrow's big, dark shape twisting and flopping around on the grass.

It was trying to get up!

"Mary-Kate! Ashley!" Samantha hollered. "Quick, get in the house!"

"No, wait! I have to find the switch!" Ashley cried. Part of the plan was for

Ashley to turn on the backyard floodlights.
"I can't find it!"

The scarecrow twisted and flopped even harder.

"Forget the lights!" Samantha shouted. I heard her footsteps pounding toward the house.

I tried to jump over the bushes, but I didn't make it. *Crash!* I landed right on top of the prickly shrubs.

"Help!" I shouted.

"Mary-Kate!" Samantha yelled.

"Aaahhh!" the scarecrow screamed.

All of a sudden the backyard lit up as bright as day. Ashley had finally found the switch. I shut my eyes against the brightness.

When I opened them, I couldn't believe it! The scarecrow was still on the ground. Scattered around it were a bunch of white sheets.

And partly buried under the scarecrow *and* the sheets was—Maggie Parker!

Before anyone could say a word, one of the upstairs windows of the Samuelses' house opened. "What is going on out there?" Samantha's mother called out. "I heard screaming. Is everybody all right?"

"We're okay, Mom!" Samantha called back. She was standing next to the picnic table. "Sorry we were so loud!"

"Well, come inside soon," Mrs. Samuels said. "It's getting late." The window slid down.

I scrambled off the bushes. "So it *was* you!" I said to Maggie.

Maggie pushed the scarecrow all the way off her and sat up. Pieces of straw were sticking to her sweater and hair. "You really scared me," she told us.

"*We* scared *you*?" Samantha asked. "What do you think you did to *us*?"

"I didn't mean to scare you," Maggie murmured. She got to her feet and picked a piece of straw from her hair. "I never thought you'd be here. What *are* you doing here, anyway?"

"We set a trap for you," Samantha said.

Ashley nodded. "We know you're the one who wrecked our decorations, Maggie."

"Ashley and I are detectives," I explained. "We figured it out."

Maggie twisted the piece of straw around her fingers. "I was mad because you didn't invite me to your party," she said. "So I decided to ruin it. But then I started to feel bad. I'm really sorry."

"If you're sorry, then why did you come here tonight?" Samantha asked. "With that…that…*thing*?"

"I was bringing the scarecrow back so you could have it for a decoration," Maggie said. She pointed to the sheets. "And I was going to hang those from the trees, like the ones you had before."

"Well, I'm glad we caught you," Ashley told her.

"Me, too," I said. "Because guess what? You *were* invited to the party!"

"Huh?" Maggie frowned. "But I didn't get an invitation."

"Mary-Kate and Ashley figured out why," Samantha said. "Patty O'Leary didn't deliver it to you!"

"Patty delivered all of them except yours," I explained.

"But it was an accident," Samantha added quickly.

"Right," I agreed. "Your invitation got buried in Patty's backpack under a ton of papers and notebooks."

Ashley giggled. "If Patty wants to be a CEO, she'd better start getting organized!"

Samantha and I laughed, too.

But Maggie sighed. "So the whole thing was just a big mix-up. I guess I should have said something at the very beginning. But I was too shy. I'm sorry."

Samantha and Ashley and I looked at

one another. I could tell we were all thinking the same thing.

"Well, this case is closed," I said. "And the party's not really ruined."

Samantha smiled at Maggie. "And you're still invited."

"I am?" Maggie asked in surprise.

"Sure," I told her. "We don't want anybody to be left out."

"That's great!" Maggie said happily. "And I really want to help get everything ready." She picked up the scarecrow. "For starters, where do you want *this*?"

On the night of our big Halloween party, the scarecrow stood propped against the big oak tree in Samantha's backyard.

Nearby was a big barrel. It was filled with water and apples. We were going to have an apple-bobbing contest later.

Everybody loved the scarecrow. Except for Patty. "You should have tossed that thing back in the Dumpster," she said with a sniff. Patty was wearing a pink ballerina costume with a tiara and toe shoes. "It's totally messed up now!"

Samantha laughed. Even if she'd frowned, it would have been hard to tell. She was dressed as a clown and had a big red smile painted on her face. "I guess the scarecrow *has* lost a lot of straw!" she said.

"That's because I dragged it around so much," Maggie said. She was a space alien. She had on a green jumpsuit and a funny hat with green balls that bobbed around on springs.

"Well, I still like it," Ashley said. She was wearing a sparkly baton-twirler outfit. I wore a tuxedo and top hat and carried a magic wand.

"Yeah, that scarecrow is pretty cool," Tim agreed from behind his rubber monster mask. "The whole party is pretty cool!" He ran off to get another handful of candy from the skull on the picnic table.

"The party is going great," I whispered to Ashley.

She nodded. "Everything looks perfect, too."

It was true. We'd worked really hard to get things ready. Maggie made a new sign and helped us hang the sheets. She also bought three new pumpkins and helped us carve them.

Even Patty had helped. When she arrived at the party, she gave us a bag of candy corn to put in the skull.

Now Patty was watching Tim. "He'd better not take *all* the candy corn," she said. "It's my favorite."

"Don't worry," I told her. "We bought some candy corn, too. And I checked to make sure that all of Maggie's spiders were gone."

Maggie stared at me. "What spiders?"

"The black rubber ones that you put

inside the skull," I reminded her.

Maggie shook her head. "I didn't put any spiders in the skull. I did a lot of other stuff, but not that."

Samantha's painted grin almost disappeared. "Then who *did*?" she asked. She looked back at the scarecrow.

The rest of us looked, too. The scarecrow still stood against the tree. It was glaring out at the yard with mean eyes.

I started to get a creepy feeling again. "Maybe this case isn't closed after all," I said.

"You're right, Mary-Kate!" Ashley suddenly cried. She pointed to one of the back windows. "Look!"

As I turned, a horrible scream filled the air. "AAAAHHH!"

Oh, no! *Another* scarecrow stood in the window!

TRICK OR TREAT!

The scarecrow's straw-filled arms waved back and forth. Its mean eyes glared. And another horrible scream came from its wide-open mouth. "AAAAAHHHH!"

Around us, all the kids at the party froze and stared at the window.

Then the scarecrow screamed a third time. And everyone started screaming with it.

"It's alive! It's ALIVE!" Tim shouted.

"I'm getting out of here!" Patty hollered.

"Everybody run!" Zach yelled.

"No, wait!" I shouted. I turned to Ashley. "We can't let him ruin the party!"

"Who?" Maggie cried. "The scarecrow?"

"Evan!" Ashley said. "It has to be Evan."

"Oh, no," Samantha said. She slapped her forehead. "Not again!"

The window suddenly opened. The scarecrow disappeared and Evan leaned out. "Gotcha!" he cried.

Everyone stopped running and stared at the window.

"That wasn't funny," Patty complained. She smoothed her ballerina tutu. "I almost twisted my ankle trying to run in these toe shoes."

"I can't believe you did that," Samantha told her brother.

"You also put the spiders in our skull, didn't you?" Ashley asked.

Evan grinned. "Hey, I can't go trick-or-treating today. I'm allowed to have *some*

kind of Halloween fun, aren't I?"

"Then we'll make a deal with you," I said. "You can come to our party. But only if you promise not to pull any more pranks on us."

Evan shrugged. "Okay, I promise," he said. "Brother's honor."

The week after our party, Ashley and Samantha and I walked home from the bus stop together.

"So has Evan played any new tricks on you?" Ashley asked Samantha.

She shook her head. "He hasn't bugged me in a while. I guess inviting him to the party worked!"

I nodded. "That's good. Everybody seemed to have a great time. Even Patty."

"Hey, isn't that the pumpkin-stand man?" Ashley asked suddenly. She pointed up ahead.

Sure enough, the bald-headed pumpkin

man stood outside another little hut. It was on a different corner this time. There were tables out in front of the hut. And they had holiday flowers and holly wreaths on them.

When the pumpkin man looked at us, he grinned. "I remember you girls," he said. "I gave you that creepy scarecrow, didn't I?"

Samantha nodded. "We came back once, but your stand was closed."

"Business is better here," the man explained. "More traffic. Say—I have just the thing for you." He reached into the hut. Then he brought out a life-size plastic snowman.

"It's a perfect holiday decoration," the man said. "No home should be without one. I can't seem to sell it, so...I'll let *you* have it for free!"

"You mean like the scarecrow?" Samantha asked slowly.

"Exactly." The man winked.

Ashley and I and Samantha glanced at each other. "Thanks!" we all said together. "But *no*, thanks!"

Hi from both of us,

Ashley and I were so excited to be part of the Jingle Bells on Ice skating show! But things went spinning out of control. The ice turned to purple slush. Skates and costumes kept disappearing. Strange music played over the loudspeaker. Some people were even saying there was a Jingle Bell Jinx.

But one thing was for sure—someone didn't want the show to go on. And it was up to us to find out who!

Want to find out more? Skate onto the next page for a sneak peek at *The New Adventures of Mary-Kate & Ashley: The Case of the Jingle Bell Jinx.*

See you next time!

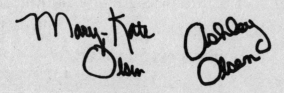

A sneak peek at our next mystery…

The Case Of The
Jingle Bell Jinx

"Somebody hid my skates!" Tina cried.

"And somebody changed my music," her sister, Terri, added.

Ashley and I sighed. We had thought we were coming to the Jingle Bells On Ice Show to see Tina and Terri skate together. But instead, we were solving a mystery!

"We'll have to stake out the rink to look for anyone suspicious," Ashley said.

"But how will we keep the culprit from spotting *us*?" I asked.

"Easy," Ashley replied. She reached into the closet. "We'll be in disguise."

I grinned as Ashley handed me a ginger-bread girl costume. "This looks good enough to eat," I joked.

Ashley zipped up her giant candy cane costume. Then she glanced in the mirror. "We look dumb," she said.

"Don't worry," Tina told her. "You'll look like all the other candies in the show."

The four of us walked over to the skating rink. The ice was crowded with gumdrops practicing sit spins.

"I hope you catch someone!" Terri called. She and Tina waved as they glided onto the ice together.

I slapped my forehead. "I forgot my binoculars in the dressing room," I said. "We can't stake out the rink without them."

"Let's run back and get them," Ashley suggested. "Terri gave me her key."

We waddled back down the hall. But when we turned the corner, we froze.

Someone was standing in front of Tina and Terri's dressing room. He was jiggling the door handle with a screwdriver.

Who was trying to break into the stars' dressing room? And why?

The Ultimate Fan'

mary-kate

Don't miss

Reading Checklist
...and **ashley**
single one!

❑ It's a Twin Thing

❑ How to Flunk
   Your First Date

❑ The Sleepover Secret

❑ One Twin Too Many

❑ To Snoop or Not to Snoop?

❑ My Sister the Supermodel

❑ Two's a Crowd

❑ Let's Party!

❑ Calling All Boys

❑ Winner Take All

❑ P. S. Wish You Were Here

❑ The Cool Club

❑ War of the Wardrobes

❑ Bye-Bye Boyfriend

❑ It's Snow Problem

❑ Likes Me, Likes Me Not

❑ Shore Thing

❑ Two for the Road

Super Specials:

❑ My Mary-Kate & Ashley Diary

❑ Our Story

❑ Passport to Paris Scrapbook

❑ Be My Valentine

THE NEW ADVENTURES OF MARY-KATE & ASHLEY™
Be a Character in a Mary-Kate & Ashley Book Sweepstakes

OFFICIAL RULES:

1. No purchase necessary.

2. To enter complete the official entry form or hand print your name, address, age, and phone number along with the words "THE NEW ADVENTURES OF MARY-KATE & ASHLEY" Be a Character in a Mary-Kate & Ashley Book Sweepstakes" on a 3"x 5" card and mail to THE NEW ADVENTURES OF MARY-KATE & ASHLEY Be a Character in a Mary-Kate & Ashley Book Sweepstakes, c/o HarperEntertainment, Attn: Children's Marketing Department, 10 East 53rd Street, New York, NY 10022, postmarked **no later than January 31, 2002**. Enter as often as you wish, but each entry must be mailed separately. One entry per envelope. Partially completed, illegible, or mechanically reproduced entries will not be accepted. Sponsor, as defined below, is not responsible for lost, late, mutilated, illegible, stolen, postage due, incomplete, or misdirected entries. All entries become the property of Dualstar Entertainment Group, Inc., and will not be returned.

3. Sweepstakes open to all legal residents of the United States (excluding Rhode Island), who are between the ages of five and fifteen by January 31, 2002, excluding employees and immediate family members of HarperCollins Publishers Inc. ("HarperCollins"), Parachute Properties and Parachute Press, Inc., and their respective subsidiaries and affiliates, officers, directors, shareholders, employees, agents, attorneys, and other representatives (individually and collectively "Parachute"), Dualstar Entertainment Group, Inc., and its subsidiaries and affiliates, officers, directors, shareholders, employees, agents, attorneys, and other representatives (individually and collectively "Dualstar"), and their respective parent companies, affiliates, subsidiaries, advertising, promotion and fulfillment agencies, and the persons with whom each of the above are domiciled. Offer void where prohibited or restricted by law.

4. Odds of winning depend on the total number of entries received. All prizes will be awarded. Winners will be randomly drawn on or about February 15, 2002, by HarperEntertainment, whose decisions are final. Potential winners will be notified by mail and will be required to sign and return an affidavit of eligibility and release of liability within 14 days of notification. Prizes won by minors will be awarded to parent or legal guardian who must sign and return all required legal documents. By acceptance of their prize, winners consent to the use of their names, photographs, likenesses, and personal information by HarperCollins, Parachute, Dualstar, and for publicity purposes without further compensation except where prohibited.

5.a) One (1) Grand Prize winner will have his or her name included in a Mary-Kate & Ashley book, as a character; and receive an autographed copy of the book in which the winner's name appears. HarperCollins, Parachute, and Dualstar reserve the right to substitute another prize of equal or greater value in the event that the winner is unable to receive the prize for any reason. Approximate retail value: $4.25.

   b) Fifty (50) First Prize winners win an autographed Mary-Kate & Ashley book. Approximate total retail value: $212.50.

6. Only one prize will be awarded per individual, family, or household. Prizes are non-transferable and cannot be sold or redeemed for cash. No cash substitute is available. Any federal, state, or local taxes are the responsibility of the winner. Sponsor may substitute prize of equal or greater value, if necessary, due to availability.

7. Additional terms: By participating, entrants agree a) to the official rules and decisions of the judges, which will be final in all respects; and to waive any claim to ambiguity of the official rules and b) to release, discharge, and hold harmless HarperCollins, Parachute, Dualstar, and their affiliates, subsidiaries, and advertising and promotion agencies from and against any and all liability or damages associated with acceptance, use, or misuse of any prize received in this sweepstakes.

8. Any dispute arising from this Sweepstakes will be determined according to the laws of the State of New York, without reference to its conflict of law principles, and the entrants consent to the personal jurisdiction of the State and Federal courts located in New York County and agree that such courts have exclusive jurisdiction over all such disputes.

9. To obtain the name of the winners, please send your request and a self-addressed stamped envelope (excluding residents of Vermont and Washington) to:

   THE NEW ADVENTURES OF MARY-KATE & ASHLEY™ Be a Character in a Mary-Kate & Ashley Book Sweepstakes
   c/o HarperEntertainment
   10 East 53rd Street, New York, NY 10022
   by March 1, 2002. Sweepstakes sponsor: HarperCollins Publishers, Inc.

Jet to London
with Mary-Kate and Ashley!

Mary-Kate Olsen Ashley Olsen

winning london

ABBEY ROAD

OXFORD ST.

winning london

DUALSTAR
VIDEO

All-new movie!

Own it on video today!

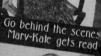

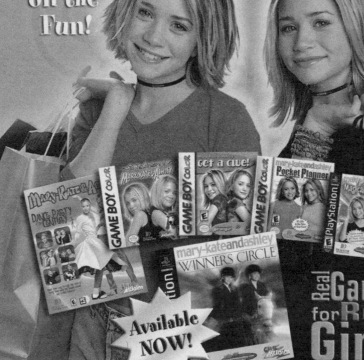